MY SPECTACULAR SELF

HEADS UP!
A RESILIENCE STORY

by Shoshana Stopek
illustrated by Gal Weizman

PICTURE WINDOW BOOKS
a capstone imprint

For Mom and Dad, who taught me to
never give up on my dreams —S.S.

Published by Picture Window Books, an imprint of Capstone
1710 Roe Crest Drive, North Mankato, Minnesota 56003
capstonepub.com

Library of Congress Cataloging-in-Publication Data
Names: Stopek, Shoshana, author. | Weizman, Gal, illustrator.
Title: Heads up! : a resilience story / by Shoshana Stopek ; illustrated by Gal Weizman.
Description: North Mankato, Minnesota : Picture Window Books, an imprint of Capstone, [2022] |
Series: My spectacular self | Audience: Ages 5-7. | Audience: Grades K-1. |
Summary: Peanut the chipmunk really wants to fly his homemade kite, but it keeps ending up on
the ground—but Peanut refuses to give up, and with the help of his animal friends the kite will fly.
Identifiers: LCCN 2021020996 (print) | LCCN 2021020997 (ebook) | ISBN 9781663984890
(hardcover) | ISBN 9781666332643 (paperback) | ISBN 9781666332650 (pdf) | ISBN 9781666332674
(kindle edition) Subjects: LCSH: Chipmunks—Juvenile fiction. | Kites—Juvenile fiction. |
Resilience (Personality trait)—Juvenile fiction. | Problem solving—Juvenile fiction. | Friendship—
Juvenile fiction. | CYAC: Resilience (Personality trait)—Fiction. | Kites—Fiction. | Problem
solving—Fiction. | Friendship—Fiction. | Chipmunks—Fiction. | Animals—Fiction. Classification:
LCC PZ7.1.S7557 He 2022 (print) | LCC PZ7.1.S7557 (ebook) | DDC 813.6 [E]—dc23
LC record available at https://lccn.loc.gov/2021020996
LC ebook record available at https://lccn.loc.gov/2021020997

Special thanks to Amber Chandler for her consulting work.

Designed by Nathan Gassman

Meet Peanut

HOBBIES: inventing, building, gardening, playing with friends

FAVORITE BOOKS: How to Train Your Robot Dog and Chipmunk Space Adventure!

FAVORITE FOODS: fruit, nuts, seeds, worms

FUTURE GOALS: to become an engineer or a pilot

GOALS FOR THIS YEAR:

-train my robot dog

-learn to fly a model airplane

-build a treehouse big enough to fit all my friends

-teach my friends how to fly a kite

Peanut was a little guy with BIG ideas
and an even BIGGER imagination.
He loved to invent . . .

and build . . .

and tend to nature.

Things didn't always go the way he planned.

But that just made him try harder. As his mama always said,
"Even when things don't work out at first, you just keep trying."

So when Peanut got his next great idea,
he couldn't wait to share it with his friends!
Naturally, they had a few questions.

"I got this," said Peanut.

"Just stand back and watch!

Ready . . . Set . . ."

Peanut tied on the bows and tried again.

and . . .

UP,

UP,

UP,

Spider wove a thread, and together they tied it.

Peanut tried again. He launched the kite and . . .

DOWN! By now, more animals had gathered around.

You need to huff and puff and blow the kite up.

But whatever Peanut did, the kite just wouldn't fly.

Maybe I'm not big enough to fly a kite, he thought.

Then he looked all around him. There was a
HUGE crowd! That gave him one more idea . . .

Carefully, Peanut climbed to the top of the pyramid.
He was taller than he had ever been before!
Surely, he could fly the kite now.

Peanut closed his eyes, took a deep breath, and let go. WHOOSH! A huge gust of wind swept through the meadow, startling the animals.

Peanut was back on the ground . . .

. . . but his kite wasn't!

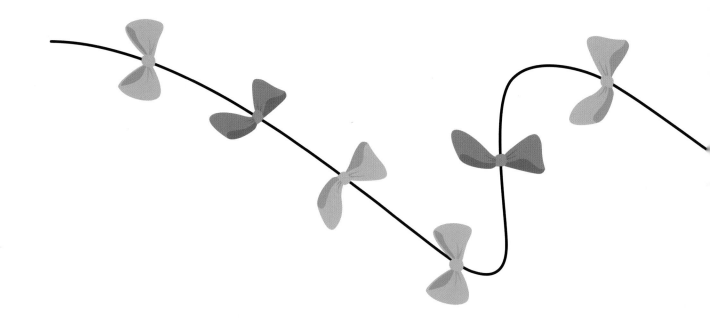

Everyone cheered as the kite soared HIGHER and HIGHER.

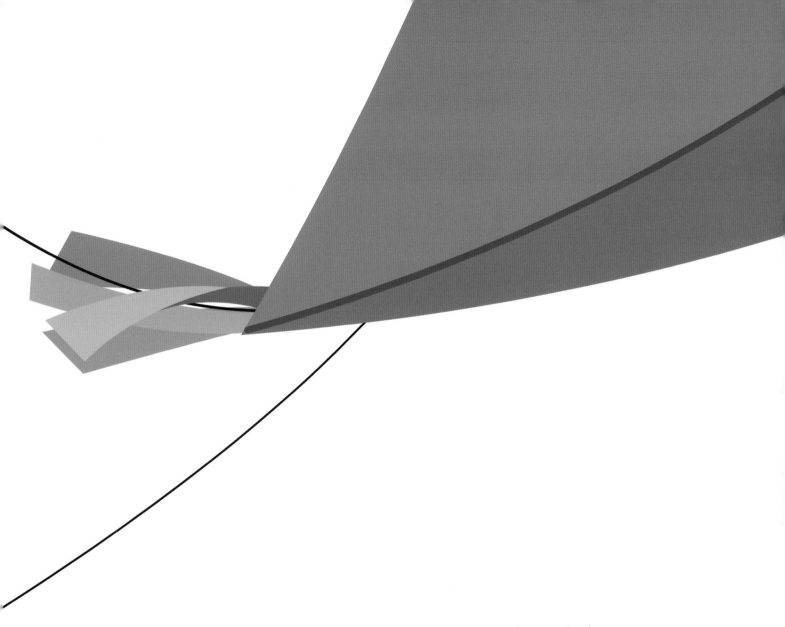

His mama was right. You just need to keep trying and always believe in yourself. And a little luck and good friends help too.

Practice Resilience

Resilience is being able to cope in a positive way when things go wrong. Repeat each of the phrases below three times. Next time you need to practice resilience, remember these sayings and believe in yourself.

I am strong.

I believe in myself.

I can do hard things.

I never give up.

I always do my best.

I can make good choices.

I am smart.

I can try new things.

Resilience Matters

1. Peanut has a big imagination. Do you have a big imagination? How can having a big imagination help you solve problems?

2. When Peanut has his idea to fly a kite, all of his friends told him the reasons it would not work. How could they be more supportive? What could they say instead?

3. Which animal in the story is your favorite? What traits does it have that make you like that character?

4. Can you list all the things that Peanut tried before the kite took off? How does this show resilience?

5. What are some encouraging words you can say to a friend who is struggling or not succeeding? Say these out loud. Practice how you say the words so that your friend will feel encouraged.

About the Author

Shoshana Stopek is the author of numerous books for kids and grown-ups. Her picture book series My Spectacular Self includes *Hammock for Two, Out-of-Control Rhino, Heads Up!,* and *Sometimes Cows Wear Polka Dots.* Shoshana grew up in New Jersey, where she learned how to make new friends, fly a kite, and bedazzle a wardrobe. Now she lives in Los Angeles with her husband and daughter where she writes and occasionally still bedazzles. Visit her at shoshanastopek.com.

About the Illustrator

Gal Welzman was born in Jerusalem, dreaming of flying above the white stone houses of her neighborhood like Peter Pan. As she grew older and became more acquainted with the laws of gravity, she had to abandon that plan. Instead, she devised a different way to never grow up: she attended Bezalel Academy of Arts and learned to draw. Gal loves to illustrate animals and creatures and to see her creations come to life. Her illustrations are bouncing through games and TV shows, sitting on packaging, and living in various children's books around the globe.